W9-BLL-830

VAMPIRE SCHOOL

Ghoul Trip

For Theo and Tara
P.B.
For my friends
C.H.

First published in Great Britain in 2010
by Boxer Books Limited.
www.boxerbooks.com

Library of Congress Cataloging-in-Publication Data
is available from the Library of Congress.
ISBN: 978-0-8075-8464-4 (hardcover)
ISBN: 978-0-8075-8465-1 (paperback)

Based on an original idea by Chris Harrison.
Text copyright © 2010 Peter Bently.
Illustrations copyright © 2010 Chris Harrison.
Published in 2011 by Albert Whitman & Company.

10 9 8 7 6 5 4 3 2 1 LB 15 14 13 12 11

For more information about Albert Whitman & Company,
visit our web site at www.albertwhitman.com.

Ghoul Trip

Written by Peter Bently
Illustrated by Chris Harrison

Albert Whitman & Company
Chicago, Illinois

Contents

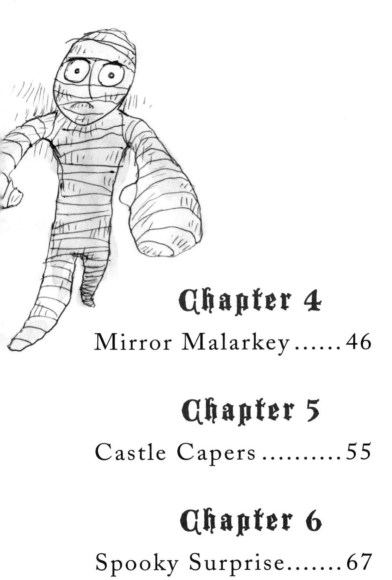

Chapter 1
A Night at the Fair

BEEP! BEEP!

Miss Gargoyle looked around at her class of young vampires. "Okay, everyone!" she said. "The school bus is here. Let's all make our way out in an orderly line!"

Lee Price stuck his hand up. "Miss Gargoyle," he asked eagerly. "Why do we have to take the bus to the county fair? Why don't we just *fly*?"

With a sudden *POP!* Lee turned into a bat and fluttered around the room.

"Yes, Miss Gargoyle, flying would be much quicker than the bus," chimed in Bella Williams.

"*And* better for the environment," added Billy Pratt. "Bats don't make smelly fumes."

"Except when they've had beans for dinner," quipped Lee.

The class burst out laughing. Even Miss Gargoyle couldn't help grinning. She was looking

forward to tonight's school
trip to the county fair just as
much as the children. When
she was a little girl, her dad
had worked on the ghost train.
She used to ride for free until
her dad got fired for being
too scary.

"We're taking the bus because it's dark and I don't want anyone to get lost on the way," she said. "Besides, I don't think it's a great idea if twenty-five bats land in the middle of the fair and

suddenly turn into a bunch of little vampires, do you? You know what Fangless folk are like. Now come along, the bus is waiting."

Lee turned back into his normal shape and followed the rest of the class out to the school bus. The side of the bus said:

St. Orlok's Elementary School

It used to say **for Vampires** too, but the school principal, Mrs. Batty, had it painted over after several terrified Fangless drivers accidentally drove into street lights.

"Come on, Billy and Bella,

let's sit at the front!" said Lee.
"Uh-oh, here's old Gore. What
does he want?"

Billy and Bella turned to

15

see Mr. E. Gore, the school janitor, hurrying across the school yard toward them.

Mr. E. Gore was not a vampire but a zombie. He was also the gloomiest, grouchiest, grumpiest, and grinchiest ghoul in town.

"Look," said Lee. "What's
that on Gore's face?"

"It looks like a new nose,"
said Bella. "It's a darker green
than his old one."

"And less warty," said Billy.
"I wonder where he got it?"

"Miss Karkoyle! Miss Karkoyle!" hollered Mr. Gore. "Shtop! Vait a moment!"

"Uh-oh," said Billy nervously. "Do you think he found that stink bomb we left in his trunk?"

"Maybe," said Lee. "But he

wouldn't dare moan about that. He was fast asleep when he should have been working."

"Miss Karkoyle!" puffed Mr. Gore glumly. "Haff you locked ze classroom?"

"No, Eric," said Miss Gargoyle coolly. "Why?"

"I must lock it at vonce!" wailed Mr. Gore. "All zese robberies in ze town! Another von just last night at Chaney Street Elementary! All ze verevolves' face brushes, stolen

during casketball practice!"
Chaney Street was the
werewolf school down the
road. "And zen last veek, at
Amenhotep High, ze spare
bandages, all shtolen! Zere
vere bits of mummies dropping
off everyvhere!"

He stroked his new nose,
which was stuck on with a
bandage.

"Aha," said Lee. "So that's
where he got it from." Amenhotep
High was the high school for
mummies.

"All zese schools being robbed!"
said Mr. Gore. "Alvays at night!

Very suspicious!" He lowered his voice to a creepy whisper that was still loud enough for everyone to hear. "D'you know sumsink, Miss Karkoyle? I know who ze robbers are!"

"Really?" said Miss Gargoyle. "Who?"

Mr. Gore nodded slyly toward her class.

"All ze robberies are at night!" he hissed. "And who comes out at night? Vampires!"

"*And* Fangless burglars," said

Miss Gargoyle firmly. "Now we *really* must get going. Goodnight, Eric!"

She climbed onto the bus and sat down.

"Crazy old ghoul," said Lee, "saying vampires might be the robbers."

"I know," said Billy. "If he hates vampires so much, why does he work in a vampire school?"

"Well," said Bella, "he couldn't get a job in a Fangless

school, could he? He'd frighten everyone to death."

"Now, now," said Miss Gargoyle. "Mr. Gore's a harmless old soul. Or he would be, if he had a soul. Anyway, tonight we're going to enjoy ourselves."

Max, the bus driver, started the engine.

"Ready, Miss Gargoyle?" he asked, fiddling with the bolt on his neck.

"You bet," she grinned. "Next stop, the county fair!"

Chapter 2
Peg Leg's Castle

The county fairgrounds were
next to a ruined castle. As
the school bus pulled up, the
vampires saw large crowds of
Fangless folk and all kinds of
brightly lit stalls and carnival
rides. There were merry-go-
rounds, a roller coaster, and

a huge Ferris wheel that was almost as tall as the castle.

"Right," said Miss Gargoyle, as the vampires filed excitedly off the bus. "While we're here I want you all to find out five things about the castle." She held up a pile of papers. "You can write them on these work sheets."

The vampires groaned.

"You mean we actually have to do some *work*?" asked Lee.

"That's right," said Miss Gargoyle. "Remember, this is a *school* trip. It's meant to be *educational*. You might live in a ruined castle yourselves one day, so it's important to know a bit about them. And the three best work sheets will each win a special prize."

"It's cool, guys," snickered Big Herb, the laziest boy in the class. "We'll just ask the castle ghosts!"

"No, you won't," said Miss Gargoyle. "First, that would be cheating. Second, there *aren't* any ghosts."

"What, a ruined castle with no ghosts?" said Big Herb in disbelief.

"Yes," said Miss Gargoyle, as she handed out the work sheets. "The castle's last owner was Peg Leg Pete, the famous pirate. He had

fifty pet parrots whose
squawking made such a
terrible racket, no one
could hear the ghosts
wailing and screeching.
So they all moved out
and never came back. See,
I've told you one thing about
the castle already. Okay, now
off you go. Enjoy yourselves."
She smiled. "Make sure you're
back at the bus
by midnight.
Don't get lost,
and don't go

flashing your fangs
or turning into bats
in front of Fangless
folk. The school
will get complaints!"

The young vampires all ran
gleefully into the fair.

"Wow!" said
Lee. "What
should we ride
on first?"

"How about the Ferris
wheel?" said Bella.

"I don't know," said Billy.
"I'm not crazy about heights."

"Oh, come on," said Lee.
"I'll pay for this one."

They joined the line for the
Ferris wheel.

"Three rides please," said
Lee, handing over some coins
to a man with shifty eyes and
a thin mustache. The man

took Lee's money and quickly
pushed the children into car
number eight.

"Hey," said Lee. "You didn't
give me any change!"

"Nonsense," sneered the man, locking them in. "Pesky kids. Have a nice ride!" He laughed nastily, and before Lee could say anything else, the Ferris wheel whisked them up into the air.

"What a cheat!" fumed Lee, glaring down at the man. "I want my money!"

"Yeah," agreed Bella. "He was *horrible*."

Just then Billy grabbed Bella's arm. They were high above the crowds now and Billy was terrified.

"Oh, dear," he quavered, shutting his eyes tight. "I can't bear to look!"

"Why don't you turn into a bat?" said Bella kindly. "You're not scared of heights when you're a bat."

"But Miss Gargoyle said we shouldn't!" said Billy.

Suddenly Lee sat up.

"Only in front of Fangless folk," he said brightly. "But when we get to the top, no one will see us."

"*Us*?" said Bella. "What do you mean, *us*?"

"I've just had an idea,"
grinned Lee. "Listen..."

Chapter 3
Bat Trick

Ten minutes later, car number seven came to a halt at the bottom of the Ferris wheel. The man with the thin mustache unlocked the door and a Fangless boy and girl got out. The wheel moved on and car number eight swung down.

"Hur-hur," sneered the man. "Here come those three weird-looking kids I cheated." He unlocked the car. It was empty. "What? Hang on a minute," he gasped. "Where'd they go?"

He looked in, under, and on top of the car. Nothing. He was baffled. Those kids had definitely got into car number eight, he was sure of it.

Or had they?

Maybe he'd got the number wrong. He waited while all the other cars came down and checked inside every one. But there was no sign of the children. He scratched his mustache, puzzled.

Finally,
car number
eight came
back down
again. The
man couldn't
understand it. Those children
had gone up, so they *must* have
come down. But where were
they? All he could see were
three little bats fluttering high
above his head.

There was a long line of
people waiting to get on the

Ferris wheel. The man thought hard.

"I'll just take one last look in car number eight," he muttered. "Maybe those pesky kids are hiding under the seat." He crawled into the car on his hands and knees for a closer look. And then three things happened very quickly.

First, the three little bats turned—*POP! POP! POP!*—into three giggling vampires.

Next, Lee quickly locked

the door of the car with a

SLAM!

Then, Billy
pressed the
green button
that said
START.

"Hey!" yelled the man.
"What's going on? Let me
out!"

But the three vampires just
smiled and waved.

"Have a nice trip," called
Lee, as car number eight

swung into the air. The man was shouting some *very* rude words, but they grew fainter and fainter as he rose higher and higher.

When car number eight reached the top of the Ferris wheel, Bella pressed the red STOP button.

"Good," said Lee. "That'll serve him right for cheating people. We'll let him out in half an hour!"

As they left the Ferris wheel, Lee hung a sign on the entrance. It said CLOSED FOR REPAIRS.

"Sorry," Lee said to the waiting Fangless people. "Come back later!"

CLOSED FOR REPAIRS

Chapter 4
Mirror Malarkey

The three vampires wandered around the fair. They bought cotton candy and ice cream, rode on the roller coaster, and guessed the weight of a large pig. They also bumped into Lee's werewolf friend Ollie Talbot and his big brother Claude. Ollie and Claude went to Chaney Street Elementary School.

"How come there's no school

tonight?" asked Lee.

"It's a blue moon," said Ollie.
"We get a night's holiday."

Ollie and Claude were
both in human form so as
not to terrify Fangless folk.
Apart from their hairy hands
they looked just like normal
children.

"We're going for a raw burger," said Ollie. "Coming?"

"No thanks," said Lee. "We just had ice cream. We're heading for the hall of mirrors."

"Okay," said Ollie. "Been on the ghost train yet?"

"No," said Lee. "Maybe we'll see you there. Fangless ghost

trains are always good for a
laugh. They're so unscary!"

Lee, Bella, and Billy had
great fun in the hall of mirrors
—until Bella stood next to a
Fangless boy who was laughing
at his weird reflection in a
wobbly mirror.

"Tee-hee!" she chuckled
along with him. "You look like
a zombie in that mirror!"

The boy stared at Bella, then
at the mirror, then at Bella
again. He stopped laughing

and his mouth fell open.

"What's wrong?" she asked. Then she realized. She had forgotten to turn her reflection on!

"Oh," she said. "Silly me! Hang on."

With a *ZZZIP!* Bella's very wide, wobbly reflection suddenly

appeared in the mirror. The
boy gaped even more.

"H-h-how d-d-d-id you d-d-
d-d-o that?" he stammered.

"Oh, it's easy," said Bella.
"We learn it at vampire
school." She smiled sweetly,
showing him her long fangs.

"AAAAAARGGGGH!"
screamed the boy. "Mom!
Dad! HEEEEEELP!" And
he shot out of the hall of
mirrors faster than you can say
Transylvania.

"What's up with him?"
asked Lee.

"I'm not sure," said Bella. "I
think it was something I said.
Maybe we'd better go."

"Yes," said Billy, looking at
his watch. "We've only got
another hour and we haven't

been on the
ghost train yet."

"Yikes!" said

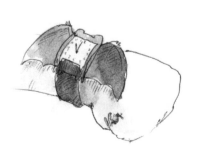

Lee. "*And* we've got Miss Gargoyle's worksheet to fill in."

"Yes," said Bella. "We'd better do that first."

The three vampires walked
to the ruined castle. But when
they got there they found the
gates chained shut and a big
sign that said:

NO ENTRY!
CASTLE HAUNTED!
NASTY GHOSTS AND
GHOULS INSIDE!
KEEP OUT!

Chapter 5
Castle Capers

"That's weird," said Lee. "Miss Gargoyle said there *weren't* any ghosts."

"Maybe they came back after all," said Bella.

"But why now?" said Billy. "Peg Leg Pete's been dead over three hundred years. The ghosts could have returned long ago."

"Hmmm," said Lee. "It's very strange. Maybe we should take a look."

"But the gates are locked!" said Billy.

"Silly Billy," said Lee. "We'll go in as bats, of course. No one'll notice. Besides, how

else can we do Miss Gargoyle's
worksheet? Come on!"

After checking to make
sure no Fangless folk were
watching, they said the bat
chant Miss Gargoyle had
taught them:

"*I'm a bat, a bat is me,*
A bat is all I want to be."

And with a *POP! POP! POP!*
they all turned into bats and
fluttered off over the castle
wall.

They flew through all the
roofless halls and ruined
chambers of the castle. It was
dark and dank and cold—and
incredibly spooky.

"Wow!" said Lee. "This place is really cool!"

"Yeah," agreed Bella. "I'll bet those old ghosts were sorry to leave!"

"No sign of any *new* ghosts, though," said Lee. "Hang on, what's that?"

They hovered over some stone steps leading down to the dungeons. At the bottom of the steps was a light!

"Uh-oh," said Billy. "It's a glowing phantom! I think we

should leave. It's not polite to enter a ghoul's home without asking."

"It's not a phantom," said Lee, peering at the light. "It's a fire. Let's take a closer look."

Lee was right. A small campfire was flickering in the dungeon. Next to it were two men.

"It's okay, they're Fangless," said Lee.

Hanging from the dungeon wall was a rusty iron chain. The vampire bats landed on it, dangled upside down, and listened.

"Where's Tony? He should be here by now," growled one of the men. He was wearing sunglasses even though it was night.

"Dunno, Jim," grunted the other man, who was as big as a truck. "The Ferris wheel stopped ages ago."

Lee grinned at Bella and Billy.

"Tony must be the guy who cheated me!" he whispered.

"Oh!" said Bella. "I'd forgotten all about him. He's still stuck at the top of the Ferris wheel!"

"But what are they doing in the castle?" wondered Billy.

He didn't have to wait long to find out.

"D'you know what, Milton?" said Jim. "If Tony doesn't show up soon, we'll just have to rob St. Orlok's without him."

"Yeah," said Jim. "We'll give him ten more minutes, then

we're outta here."

The vampire bats nearly fell off their chain. So that was it! The three men were the robbers who'd been burglarizing the local schools. And the castle was their hideout!

"So that's why we haven't met a single ghost," said Lee.

"There aren't any!"

"Yes," agreed Bella. "That sign on the castle gate is just a trick to keep everyone away."

"We should tell the Fangless police," said Lee.

"But the men will be gone by the time they get here!" said Billy.

"You're right," said Bella. "We'll have to make sure they don't get away. But how?"

They dangled in silence for a minute. Then Lee spoke.

"I've got an idea," he said, flitting into the air. "I'll explain when I get back. You stay here and keep an eye on the men."

"But where are you going?" cried Bella.

"First I'm going to see Miss Gargoyle," said Lee. "Then I need to find Ollie and Claude..."

Chapter 6
Spooky Surprises

Lee quickly flew off while Billy and Bella hung in the darkness, watching the men.

After about ten minutes, Billy said, "Brrr! I wish Lee would hurry up. I'm getting cold. And bored!"

Just then the man called Milton took off his sunglasses and looked at his watch.

"Shh!" whispered Bella. "He's saying something."

"Okay. Tony's not here," said the man. "So we're going to have to do it without him."

"Right," agreed the man called Jim. "You got all the tools for breaking in?"

"In the truck with the loot," said the first man. "It's parked at the back of the castle."

"Good," said the other man.
"Let's go."

Billy and Bella looked at each other in alarm.

"Oh no!" said Billy. "We've got to stop them! But how?"

"There's only one thing to do," said Bella.

"You don't mean...?" gasped Billy.

"Yup," said Bella.

"The full vampire works."

"What, fangs and all?" Billy asked.

"Yup. Fangs and all."

"But—but Miss Gargoyle said we shouldn't!" said Billy. "It's against school rules!"

"Look," said Bella. "This is an emergency, right? Miss Gargoyle will understand. It's the only way!"

The two men stood up to go.

"Quick!" said Bella. "You

go and flap in their faces.
That should slow them down.
Hurry!"

Billy didn't need to be asked
twice. The men had almost
reached the dungeon steps.
The man called Milton was in
front. Billy flew straight at his
head, giving his hair a good
ruffling.

"Urgh!" cried the man,
stopping so suddenly that the

other man barged right into him. They both tumbled to the ground in a heap.

"Oof!" grunted the second man, picking himself up. "You dummy, Milt! What's the matter?"

"N-nothing," said the first man. "A bat, I think."

The man called Jim snickered.

"Scared of a tiny bat? You'll be seeing *vampires* next, hur-hur!"

"Okay!" whispered Bella, fluttering over to join Billy in the shadows. "I'll go first."

A few seconds later there was a *POP!*

The noise made both men jump. They squinted in the dark.

"Jim?" whispered the first man. "Look—over there, in the corner! What's that?"

"I-I dunno, Milt," shivered the other man.

Bella's dark shape was moving silently toward them. She was quite short, but the shadows from the fire made her look much bigger.

POP!

Another shape appeared in the firelight.

"Hey!" said the man called Milton. "What's going on? Who are you?"

"They *look* human," muttered

the other man. "B-but what
are they wearing? Looks like
some sort of cape."

Staring their scariest stares,
Billy and Bella got closer
and closer and stopped. Then
they slowly raised their arms,
opened their capes, and

grinned a pair of huge fangy
grins.

"Arrrrrggghhhh! Vampires!
Run!"

The men bolted up the
dungeon steps. They hurtled
across a courtyard, through
a ruined hall, and out to the
back of the castle, where their
truck was waiting. Billy and
Bella arrived just in time to
see them suddenly screech to a
halt. In front of the truck sat a
very large dog.

"Hey!" said Milton. "Whose mutt is this? Here boy! Good boy!"

SNARRRRRLLLLL!

Milton hastily backed away.

"Okay, okay!" he said nervously. "N-nice doggy!"

The dog stood on its hind legs and stared at them with big yellow eyes.

It snarled again,
then lifted its
snout and went,
"HOOOOOOOWWLLLL!"
"D-doggy?" stuttered Jim.
"That ain't no dog, Milt.
That's a...
WEREWOLF!
AAAARRRGGHHH!"

The two men ran for their lives, with the werewolf in hot pursuit. Billy and Bella were about to follow when a bat flew down to join them.

It was Lee. He turned back into a vampire with a *POP!*

"Nice work, you two!" he said. "Ollie's going to chase

them to the front gate. Come on!"

The two men didn't stop running till they reached the gate with the sign on it about ghosts and ghouls.

"Darn it, I forgot we locked it!" cried Jim. "Quick, Milt, gimme the key before those monsters get here!"

"*You've* got the key," cried Milton.

"I gave it to *you*!"

"No, Milt, I gave it to
you, you numbskull!"

"Did not!"

"Did too!"

SNAAAARRRRLLLL!
HOOOOOOOOWLLL!

The men spun round. The
werewolf! And now THREE
vampires!

Then, out of the shadows by
the gatepost, something else
appeared. It had its arms out
in front and it was wrapped in
bandages. And it was stomping

toward them, moaning.

"Yowee! A mummy! ARRRGHHH!"

The two robbers kicked and bashed at the gate until it finally burst open and they ran out—straight into the arms of the police.

A police captain stepped forward, with Miss Gargoyle beside him.

"Well, well!" said the captain. "If it isn't Milton Grobble and Jim Snark. We've been looking for you for ages. We want to ask you about a few robberies."

"It was us! It was us," wailed Jim. "Just save us from those horrible ghouls!"

"Please, put us in jail!" begged Milton. "The strongest

one you got! Anywhere away from those monsters!"

"Monsters?" said the captain. "What monsters?"

"There!" said Milton. "Right behind us!"

"Nice try, guys," laughed the captain. "Hi, kids."

Puzzled, the two robbers slowly turned around. There stood five children—Lee, Bella, Billy, Ollie, and Claude.

"Well done, kids," said the captain. "Your teacher told us where to wait. Now we just

need to find Tony Kreep, the
third member of the gang."

Lee, Billy, and Bella laughed.

"He's at the top of the Ferris
wheel," said Lee. "And all the
loot is in their truck, behind
the castle."

"Excellent," said the captain.

He looked at the vampire
children and Miss Gargoyle.
"Hey, great costumes, by
the way. Been to a costume
party?"

"Something like that,"
grinned Bella. This time she
was careful *not* to show her
fangs.

The police captain turned to

Milton and Jim. "Monsters, huh? Scared of a bunch of kids!"

All the police officers laughed.

"B-but there *were* monsters!" groaned Milton. "Honest!"

"Tell that to the judge," said the captain. "Take them away, sergeant."

"The robbers wanted everyone else to think the castle was haunted," said Lee as they got back on the bus. "So I thought *they* might as well think so, too!"

"It was great of Ollie and Claude to help out," said Bella. "Claude was a fantastic mummy! Where did he get those bandages?"

"I borrowed them from the first aid tent," said Lee.

"Fangtastic!" said Billy.

"Thanks," said Lee. "You and Bella were fangtastic, too."

"Well," said Miss Gargoyle. "You three certainly discovered a few interesting things about that castle! I think you deserve the prizes. Don't you agree class?"

The whole bus cheered as Miss Gargoyle handed an envelope each to Lee, Bella, and Billy. They opened them and gasped in delight.

"Wow!" said Lee. "A ticket to the circus!"

"Doctor Acula's Vampire Spectacula!" cried Bella. "I *so* wanted to see his show!"

"Me, too," said Billy. "But it's been sold out for months!"

They all chorused, "Thanks, Miss Gargoyle!" as Max started the bus and headed back to St. Orlok's School.

Hungry for more?

Sink your teeth into the next
Vampire School adventure.

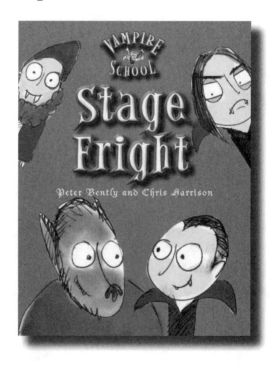

Here's a sneak peek!

Chapter 1

Ghoul Show

The school clock was striking
nine when a small bat zoomed
up to the main entrance of
St. Orlok's Primary School.
The bat hovered in front of the
doors for a moment, then with
a POP! it turned into a boy. It
was Lee Price, and he was late
for school. Vampire school.

Lee dashed through the doors
—and almost crashed right
into Mr. E. Gore, the school
caretaker.

"Hey! Votch vere you're
going!" grumbled Mr Gore.

"Sorry!" called Lee, speeding
down the corridor with his
black cape flapping behind him.

"Late again, huh?" yelled
Mr. Gore.

He shook his fist so hard that little flakes of rotten skin flew off it like green dandruff. "Pesky vampire kids! So unreliable! Ve zombies are alvays dead on time!"

Lee reached his classroom and burst in just as his teacher, Miss Gargoyle, was taking the register. All the other young vampires turned to stare at him.

"Sorry I'm late, Miss!" he gasped breathlessly, plonking himself down at a table next

to his friends Billy Pratt and
Bella Williams.

"Really, Lee," sighed Miss
Gargoyle. She peered at the
clock. "I nearly marked you
absent. Tonight of all nights!"